To my family and friends for
enduring my interruptions
and tantrums.—M.M.

Philomel Books
an imprint of Penguin Random House LLC
375 Hudson Street
New York, NY 10014

Copyright © 2019 by Mike Malbrough.

Library of Congress Cataloging-in-Publication Data
Names: Malbrough, Mike, author, illustrator.
Title: Marigold finds the magic words: a please and thank you story / Mike Malbrough.
Description: New York, NY: Philomel Books, an imprint of Penguin Random House LLC, [2019]
Summary: When party-crashing birds ruin Marigold's magic act during his
otherwise perfect birthday party, he makes all of his guests disappear before
recalling the magic words to bring them back.
Identifiers: LCCN 2018018994 | ISBN 9781524737436 (hardback) | ISBN 9781524737467 (ebook)
Subjects: | CYAC: Birthdays—Fiction. | Parties—Fiction. | Magic tricks—Fiction. | Behavior—Fiction.
| Cats—Fiction. | Birds—Fiction. | Perfectionism (Personality trait)—Fiction. | BISAC: JUVENILE
FICTION / Animals / Cats. | JUVENILE FICTION / Holidays & Celebrations / Birthdays. | JUVENILE
FICTION / Humorous Stories.
Classification: LCC PZ7.1.M34695 Mav 2019 | DDC [E]—dc23
LC record available at https://lccn.loc.gov/2018018994

Manufactured in China by RR Donnelley Asia Printing Solutions Ltd.
ISBN 9781524737436
1 3 5 7 9 10 8 6 4 2

Edited by Michael Green.
Design by Ellice M. Lee.
Text set in Museo.
The art was done in watercolor.

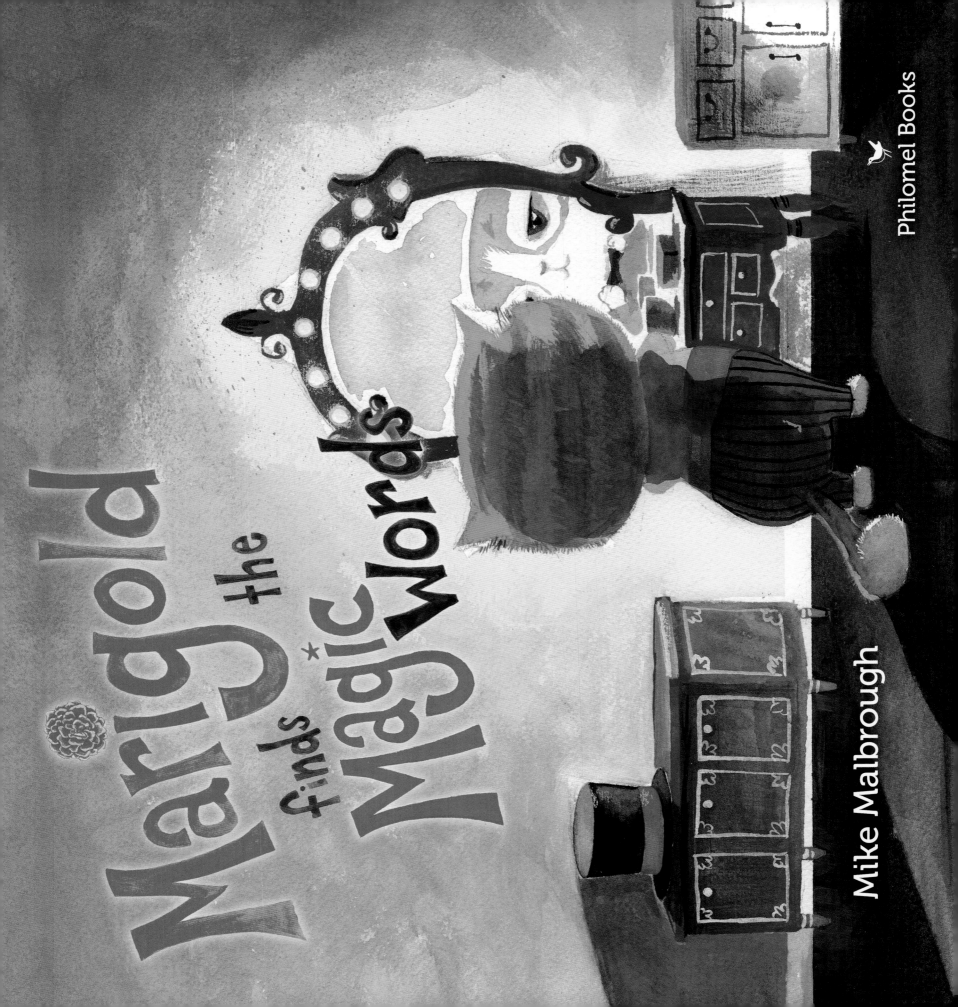

Marigold the finds Magic Words

Mike Malbrough

Philomel Books

Marigold hosted the best parties.

He planned well in advance, baked himself a very impressive birthday cake, and always had something up his sleeve!

His guests expected nothing less.

So when everyone gathered for Marigold's birthday, they were ready for something exciting.

Something extraordinary.

Something . . .

. . . magical.

Or,
with
a few
frisky
flourishes,
turn one
rainbow
ring . . . .

. . . into many, many, many more.

Marigold had practiced for
months, learning all the tricks
any magician should know.

With a snap of his fuzzy paw,
he could turn a handkerchief
into a magic wand.

It was sure to
DAZZLE and
AMAZE,

One trick, however,
was Marigold's
FAVORITE.

Marigold loved to make things VANISH, VAMOOSE, and . . .

and was perfect for a puss who liked everything just so.

disappear?

But for some reason, the trick wasn't working.

"Mr. Finch," Marigold said, "what are you doing here?"

Mr. Finch did not reply.

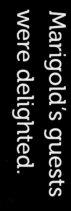

Marigold's guests
were delighted.

They thought the magic
act was funny.

But Marigold was MIFFED.

He trapped Mr. Finch in his box and tried some more magic words.

"Roasted quail and chicken soup, make this meddler

FLY THE COOP!"

SNAP

But when Marigold lifted the lid to take a peek . . . .

. . . out popped a pair
of prancing pigeons!

His audience
giggled and
guffawed.

Marigold quickly crammed the birds into the credenza.

"Chocolate-covered finches! Pigeons on sticks! Unwanted interlopers . . .

HIT THE BRICKS!"

Marigold carefully opened the doors . . .

"Oh no!"

"Three sequined seagulls?!" he said.

His friends roared with laughter.

Marigold howled,

"THAT'S NOT RIGHT!"

These magic
words had
to be the
right ones.

He corraled the
cockamamie
critters into his
vanishing cabinet
and gathered
himself for one
final try.

Marigold raised his wand and commanded.

Something
disappeared,
all right.

Marigold's friends rose to their feet and erupted in applause. But Marigold was angry enough . . .

. . . to bring the house down!

"STOP ALL YOUR CLAPPING!"

he cried, clawing down the curtains.

"STOP ALL YOUR FLAPPING!"

he yelled as he leapt onto the lights.

"This is MY STAGE! MY SHOW! MY BIRTHDAY! And I want EVERYONE to DISAPPEAR — PLEASE!"

which they did.

"I must be the best magician ever to pull off a great trick like that," Marigold thought, trying to catch his breath.

He looked at the empty room. He looked at his magnificent birthday cake . . . and decided that celebrations weren't much fun without anyone to share them with.

So he slobbered out some simple words—

"THANK YOU FOR COMING TO MY PARTY!"

and

"PLEASE COME BACK!"

—and hoped they were magic
enough to bring his friends back.

They were.

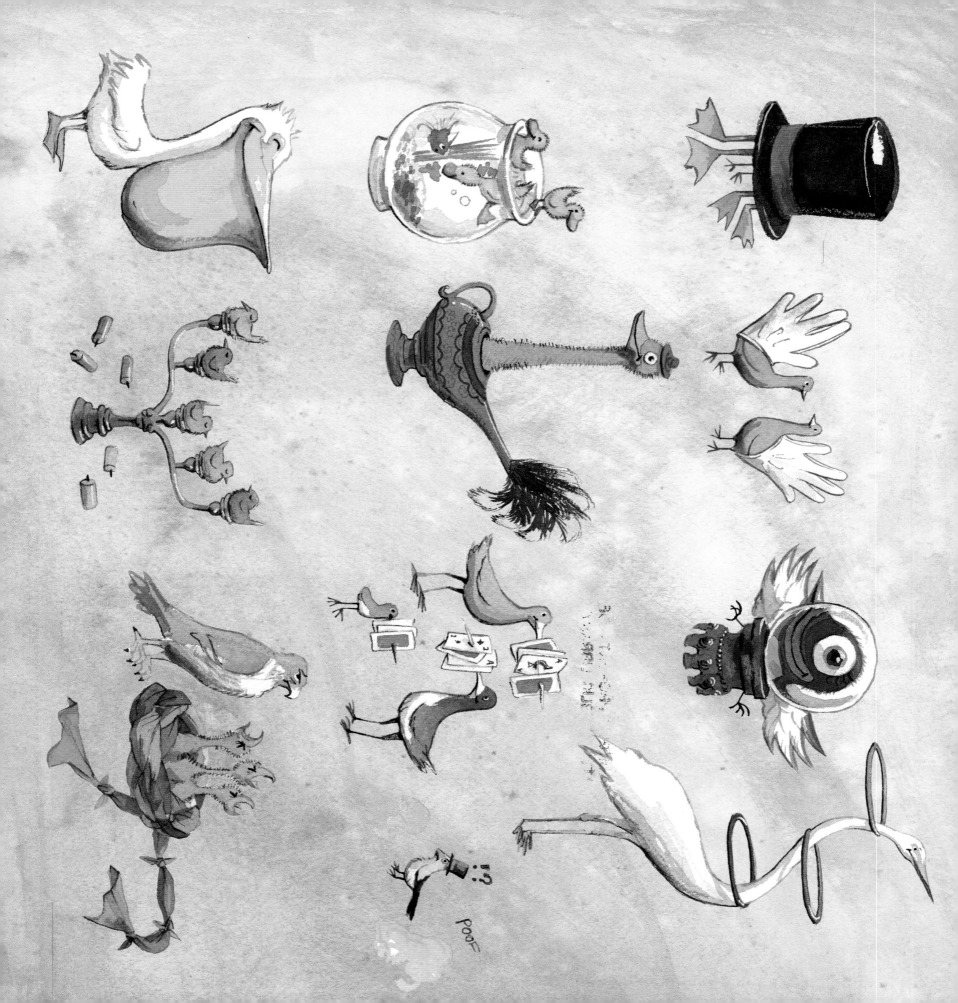

POOF